Peppa Pig™

Stars

It is almost time for bed. Mummy Pig, Daddy Pig and Peppa are having mugs of hot milk. "Snort! Snort!" George comes running in wearing his spacesuit!

"George! Why are you in that spacesuit?" asks Daddy.

"You should be in your pyjamas!"

"Hee! Hee! Snort! Snort!"

George loves everything to do with space.

Clunk! Clunk! Oh dear! George
is trying to drink through his helmet.
"George!" cries Peppa. "Take your space
helmet off to drink your milk."

Peppa takes George's helmet off.
Slurp! Slurp! Burp! That's better!
"It's bedtime, little ones!"
calls Daddy Pig.

Peppa and George are tucked up in bed. George likes to listen to his space mobile. "Not space again!" sighs Peppa. "It's boring!"
"Space isn't boring, Peppa. It's full of wonderful stars!" smiles Daddy Pig.

"Snort! I can't see anything," says Peppa, looking out of the bedroom window. "It's easier to see the stars outside," explains Daddy Pig. "If you put your coats on, we could go and see."

"That one is the North Star," says Daddy Pig.
Peppa sings a star song, "North Star! North Star! Are you
near, or are you far? Can we get there in the car?"
"The stars are too far to get to by car, but they look
closer through a telescope," replies Daddy.
"Grandpa Pig has a telescope," says Mummy Pig.
"It's late, but we can drive to his house, just this once."

Peppa and George have arrived at
Granny and Grandpa Pig's house.
Mummy Pig rings the doorbell. Ding! Dong!
"What are you doing here?" asks Grandpa.

"Could we take a look through your telescope, please?" asks Mummy Pig.
"Very well," replies Grandpa. "To the top of the house we go!"

Grandpa Pig's hobby is looking at the stars.
"Snort! Here she is! Old Bess!" says Grandpa Pig.
"Wow!" gasps Peppa, seeing the telescope.
"Who's for the first look?" asks Grandpa.
"Me, me, me!" shouts Peppa.

"It's the North Star!" cries Peppa. "We sailors use that star to find our way home," explains Grandpa Pig. "Daddy used it to find his way here," Peppa adds, smiling.

Now, it is George's turn to look through the telescope. He can see a planet with rings. "Snort! What else is in the sky?" asks Peppa. "George can see the planet Saturn," says Grandpa. "What is Saturn like?" cries Peppa.

"Saturn has rings made of rock and ice and it is very, very cold!" says Grandpa Pig. "We could build a snowman!" cries Peppa. "Quick! Look, Peppa!" gasps Grandpa. "It's a shooting star. You have to make a wish . . ."

"I wish that when George is old enough to have his own rocket, he will take me into space!" cheers Peppa, happily. "Snort! Snort!" grunts George. "Ha ha! Snort!" Everyone laughs!

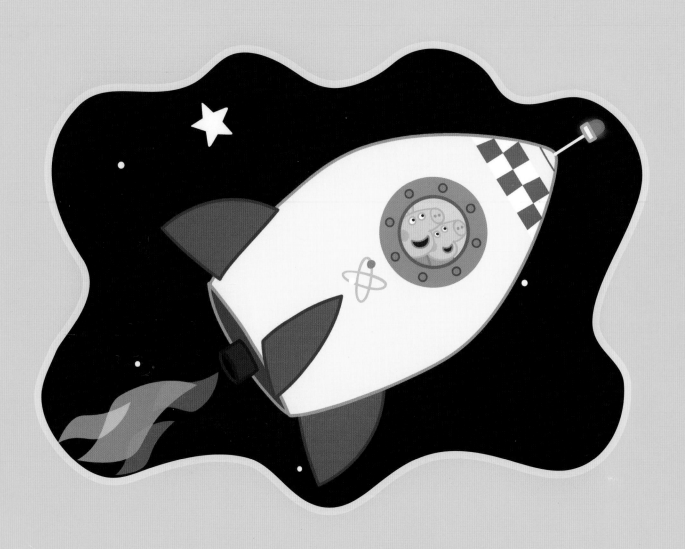